Advent Angels

Text copyright © Sue Doggett 1999
Illustrations copyright © Francis Blake 1999

Published by
The Bible Reading Fellowship
Ist Floor, Elsfield Hall,
15–17 Elsfield Way, Oxford OX2 5FG

ISBN 1 84101 099 5

First published 1999
1 3 5 7 9 10 8 6 4 2

Acknowledgments
Scriptures quoted from the Good News Bible published by The Bible Societies/HarperCollins Publishers
Ltd, UK © American Bible Society 1966, 1971, 1976, 1992, used with permission.

p.44: *True Love*, Words and Music by Cole Porter, © 1973 Cole Porter/Buxton-Hill-Music Corp,
Warner/Chappell Music Ltd, London W6 8BS. Extract reproduced by permission of International Music
Publications Ltd.

A catalogue record for this book is available from the British Library

Printed and bound in Malta by Interprint Ltd

Advent
Angels

A host of stories, crafts, puzzles and things to do for the days of Advent

Sue Doggett

Includes photocopy permission for the craft illustrations

Auras of light

News-bearing beings

Guardian friends

Eloquent singers

Lyrical messengers

Servants of God

4

How to use this book

First of all, read the story *A pocket full of angels*. Next, join George and Stephanie day by day as they listen to stories of Advent angels. Each story is followed by a suggestion of things to think about and do, and a prayer for you to use. Make sure you look out for the angel object at the top of the page.

For the Christmas tree decoration, photocopy the basic angel shape on page 63 on to card. You'll need twenty-four all together, but you don't need to make them all at once. Colour and decorate each angel as you go along. You will also need to photocopy the angel objects on pages 60–62 and stick them on to card. When you've read a story, find the angel object from the story. Cut out the shape and colour it in. Fit it into the slots on the front of the angel shape. Use a hole punch to make a hole at the top of the angel and tie a loop of thread through the hole. Hang the angel on your Christmas tree.

The basic angel shape is also used in some of the craft activities. Others use the small angel shape on page 64.

If you are unable to photocopy on to card, photocopy on to paper and then stick on to card before cutting out.

Instructions to make your very own Advent Angel can be found on pages 58–59.

A pocket full of angels

It was the day of the Christmas fair. Teachers, pupils and parents had been busy all morning transforming the school hall from its everyday self into a promise of delights.

A flurry of silver stars hung from the ceiling. Glittering twists of tinsel wound their way down the staircase and along the edges of the gift-laden tables. Shimmering lanterns and puffy paper garlands were looped between the climbing-bars and the equipment cupboards on either side of the room.

A magnificent Christmas tree stood proudly at the head of the stairs leading down into the hall. Year 6 had spent a busy Friday afternoon carefully unwrapping tissue-clad baubles for its branches and piling soft toys, boxed games, paint sets, books and warm woollen hats, gloves and scarves around its base. These were the gifts each class had collected for children who didn't have such things to look forward to at Christmas.

George came through the front door with his mum and his big sister, Stephanie. He didn't often use the main entrance and a tinge of excitement crept into his tummy as he entered the building. His nose was greeted with the smell of Christmas: pine-green needles and rich-fruited pies. His eyes widened at the sight of the tree with its shining baubles, coloured lights and nest of toys. His fingers traced the shape of the coins in his pocket.

The school fair marked the beginning of Christmas. George loved Christmas. At the far end of the hall stood a large, round tub covered in red crêpe paper. Yellow sawdust was spilling over the sides and on to the floor. '30 pence a go, two goes for 50 pence,' said the lady sitting beside the tub. It was Mrs Miller, one of the dinner ladies. She smiled at George.

George peered inside. 'What will I win, Mrs Miller?' he asked.

'A surprise!'

George dug his hand deep into his pocket. His fingers closed around one of the fat pound coins.

'I'll have two goes, then,' he said.

Mrs Miller gave him 50 pence in exchange for his coin. George pulled up his sleeve and buried his arm into the scratchy, dry depths of the tub. The sawdust spilt around his feet as his hand searched for a prize. At last his fingers curled around something hard and round. He pulled it out and ripped off the paper. A tiny wooden yo-yo lay in his hand. Cool!

'Thanks, Mrs Miller!' He turned to show his prize to Stephanie, who was browsing amongst the books and dolls.

'Don't forget your second go!'

George had forgotten. Putting the yo-yo into his pocket, again he plunged his hand into the scrunchy wooden chips. Once more his fingers gripped a prize. This time it felt softer, and not so tightly wrapped. George pulled off the paper. In the palm of his hand lay the prettiest doll he had ever seen. She was dressed in a cloud of pearly silk. A web of lace-white wings sprang from her shoulders. A tiny circle of stiffly twisted thread cast a golden light above her brow.

George gasped and looked at Mrs Miller.

'Why, it's the angel for the top of the tree!' she exclaimed. 'How did she get in there?'

George's face fell. Wasn't he to win her after all?

'You won her fair and square, George. It wasn't your fault she got into the bran tub.'

Mrs Miller smiled kindly at George. 'Off you go, now. And take good care of her—angels are very special.'

George suddenly had a thought. Taking his hanky from his pocket, he carefully wrapped the angel in its folds. Then he buried her in the safe and secret darkness of his pocket.

'Mum, why are angels special?'

George and Stephanie were enjoying a fireside tea after their busy afternoon at the fair. George helped himself to half a hot buttered bun and drizzled golden syrup over it as he asked the question.

'Angels are God's special messengers, George,' replied Mum, keeping her eye on the syrup. 'Why do you ask?'

George told Mum about the bran tub angel. He pulled his hanky from his pocket and carefully unwrapped his prize.

'She could go on top of *our* Christmas tree, couldn't she?'

George smiled at Mum. That was exactly what he had thought.

'I'll tell you what, George, it's the first day of Advent tomorrow. We'll read an angel story every day as we wait for Christmas to come. They'll be our special Advent angels. We'll hang them on our tree, with your bran tub angel at the very top.'

George and Stephanie looked at each other.

'Are there lots of angels, then?' The question came from both of them at once.

'Indeed there are,' said Mum.

'It'll be like having a pocket full of angels, George,' said Stephanie.

And it was...

Angels for lunch

FROM GENESIS 18:1–15

Next morning, nothing more was said about the Advent angels and the family went off to church. When they got home, a delicious smell greeted them as they walked in the door. Mum had made a tasty stew. A loaf of fresh bread and a jug of milk stood ready on the table.

'Time for our first Advent angels!' said Mum. 'We'll start with the story of Abraham—it reminds us of something that was said in the Christmas story.

'Abraham lived in a very hot country. His home was a tent. One day, he was sitting in the entrance of his tent. It was the hottest part of the day and he was dozing in the shade.

'Suddenly he looked up and saw three men walking towards him. Abraham jumped up and ran out to meet his visitors. He made them comfortable and brought water so that they could wash their dusty feet. Then he hurried into the tent and called out to his wife, Sarah, to prepare a meal of fresh bread, tasty stew and creamy milk.

'Abraham set the food in the shade of a tree. As they were eating, one of the visitors turned to Abraham and asked him where Sarah was. She was in the tent, of course!

'"Sarah's going to have a baby boy," said the visitor.

'Sarah was standing just inside the door of the tent and she heard what the man said. She laughed quietly to herself. Impossible! She was far too old!

'"Why are you laughing, Sarah?" the man called out. Sarah gasped. He must have read her thoughts! She felt her cheeks go red. She had always wanted a baby!

'The man spoke again. "Is anything too hard for the Lord?"

'Abraham stared at his visitors. These were no ordinary men. They were angels! He had invited angels to lunch!

'This special message was also given to Mary when the angel came to tell her that she was going to be Jesus' mother,' Mum said.

'She opened George's picture Bible to show them.

 There is nothing that God cannot do.
LUKE 1:37

To do

Next time you lay the table, set an extra place and tell the story of Abraham and the angels. Draw a picture of the loaf of bread, pot of stew and jug of milk and use it instead of the place mat. It will need to be laminated if you want to put hot plates on it. You can get this done at your local office suppliers.

 Dear Lord, thank you that everything is possible for you. Amen

Angels on the stairs

FROM GENESIS 28:10–17

Next morning, George woke up with a start. He could feel something hard beneath his head. He pushed his hand under the pillow. A stone! How did that get there? Just at that moment Stephanie came into the room. She, too, had found a stone under her pillow.

At breakfast, George's picture Bible was lying open on the table.

'Today's angel reminds us of a promise God made in the Christmas story,' said Mum, as she joined them at the table.

'One of Abraham's grandsons was called Jacob. One day, when he was a teenager, Jacob quarrelled with his brother, Esau. The quarrel was so bad that Jacob left home to live with his uncle. He felt very lonely as he set out on the long journey. That night he lay down to sleep, resting his head on a stone.

'Jacob began to dream—perhaps his stone pillow kept him from sleeping soundly. In his dream he saw a stairway that reached from earth to heaven. Angels were going up and down the stairs. And God was standing beside him.

'God told Jacob how much he loved him. He promised to look after Jacob. He promised to be with him always.

'Jacob woke up. He no longer felt alone. God had been with him all the time, even though he hadn't realized it! He took the stone pillow and set it on the ground as a reminder of that special place where he had met God.

'This important message is also in the Christmas story,' Mum said.

She opened the Bible to show them.

 The angel came to Mary and said, 'The Lord is with you.'
LUKE 1:28

To do

Find a large, smooth, round stone. Wash and dry it. Draw a picture from the story or write the angel's words on the surface of your stone.

 Thank you, heavenly Father, that you are always with us. Amen

The rough-and-tumble angel

FROM GENESIS 32:22—33:4

'What has Jacob got to do with Christmas?'

George was just putting the finishing touches to his stone. There was paint on the tip of his nose. He swirled his brush in a jar of water and watched the clear liquid turn bright blue.

'Jacob loved God,' replied Mum. 'And Jesus is king of everyone who loves God. Jacob is part of the path that leads to the Christmas story.

'Many years after Jacob had quarrelled with his brother, he decided to go back home and say sorry. He was afraid that Esau would still be angry with him, so he thought he would try to win him over with expensive presents.

'On the way home, Jacob got into a fight. It was dark and Jacob didn't realize that the man he was fighting with was really an angel. What a rough-and-tumble they had! Jacob was determined to win. They wrestled with each other right through the night. As day began to break, the angel struck Jacob on the hip so that he would have to let go. But still Jacob clung on. He wanted to know the man's name. But the man wouldn't say. Instead, he blessed Jacob.

14

'Suddenly, Jacob realized that he had been fighting with God. Once again God had been with him—even though Jacob hadn't realized it! Later that day, Jacob met his brother. Esau ran to meet him and they forgave each other. The struggle was over!'

'What a lovely present!' said George.

Mum smiled. 'There is a message about Jacob in the Christmas story,' she said. She opened the Bible to show him where.

 'Jesus will be the king of the descendants of Jacob for ever.'
LUKE 1:33

To do

Wrap a Christmas present for someone you want to say 'sorry' to.

Make a card tag using the small angel shape on page 64.

 Thank you, Lord Jesus, for the present of your love. Amen

An angel in the bush

FROM EXODUS 3:1–12

The next morning, George woke up with a temperature. Mum felt his head.

'No school for you today, George.' She tucked him back into bed and called the doctor. George felt hot and miserable. It was football today. He was in the school team. He didn't want to miss out.

The doctor came. He left some medicine for George to take. George sighed and went to sleep. When he woke up, Mum was sitting on the edge of the bed. She was cutting something out of red card. A twig was lying on the duvet.

'Hello, George,' she said. 'I thought we'd have a hot angel story today.' George sat up in bed. He felt a little bit better.

'It was a hot, hot day. Moses the shepherd was looking after the sheep and goats. He led the flock across the desert and on to the mountainside. Thin, dry grass grew through the sandy soil. A hot breeze rustled the brown leaves on the dry bushes. Moses wiped his brow. Phew! This was hard work.

'Suddenly, above the bleating of the sheep, he heard the sound of crackling. One of the bushes was on fire! He could see the flames, but the bush wasn't burning up. Moses went to take a closer look.

'"Moses, Moses."

'There was an angel in the bush! An angel with a hot message for Moses! God wanted someone to lead his people out of Egypt, across the desert and into the land where he wanted them to live. Phew! This was even harder work!

'Moses was just an ordinary person. But God helped him to do this special job.'

Mum smiled. 'The Christmas story tells us that Mary was just an ordinary person, too,' she said.

She opened George's Bible to show him.

 'I am the Lord's servant,' said Mary; 'may it happen to me as you have said.'
LUKE 1:38

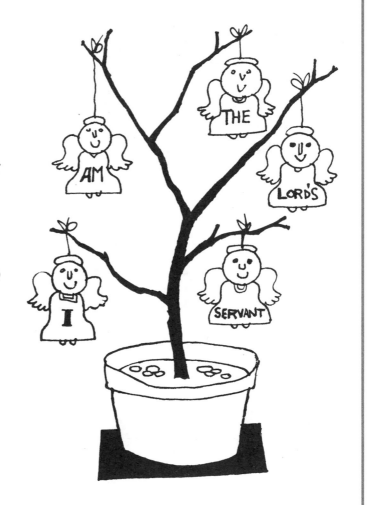

To do

• Find a strong, dry twig with at least five branches on it.

• Paint it red with poster paint. When the paint is dry, 'plant' your twig in a flowerpot full of earth.

• Cut five small angel shapes out of red card. Make a hole in the top of each. Write the words *I am the Lord's servant* individually on the angels (one word on each angel).

• Slip some thread through the hole and tie each angel to your 'burning bush' model.

 Dear God, help us to trust you. Amen

Angel food

FROM EXODUS 16:1–36

George was getting better. His throat still felt very sore, but that didn't stop him getting hungry! It made him feel very grumpy.

Stephanie had played games with him when she came home from school, but then she'd gone off to watch her favourite television programme. Mum was in the kitchen, cooking tea.

'Here I am, hungry and thirsty and all on my own,' grumbled George, 'and nobody cares!'

The door opened and in walked Mum. She was carrying a tray. Something smelt very good indeed.

'Not grumbling, are we, George?' She set the tray down beside the bed. 'I've brought you some angel food, but I think I'll tell you a grumbly story to go with it!

'Moses did what God asked him to do. He led the people out of Egypt and into the desert. The desert was big and hot and dusty. Soon everyone was hot and grumpy. They were tired and hungry. Did nobody care? They grumbled at Moses. They forgot that Moses had rescued them from their awful life in Egypt.

'"When you grumble at me, you are really grumbling at God," said Moses. "But he will help you."

'That evening there was a tasty quail supper for tea. In the morning, delicious bread!'

Mum watched while George ate his supper. 'You would have thought that Mary and Joseph had a lot to grumble about,' she said, 'but they just made the best of what they had.'

She opened George's Bible to show him.

While they were in Bethlehem, the time came for Mary to have her baby. She gave birth to her first son, wrapped him in strips of cloth and laid him in a manger—because there was no room for them to stay in the inn.
LUKE 2:6–7

To do

Ask an adult to help you make George's angel food.

- Heat 25g of butter in a saucepan with 140ml of milk.
- Add 50g of fresh breadcrumbs and 50g of grated cheese.
- When the cheese has melted, add a beaten egg and stir until the egg is cooked.
- Serve with thinly sliced and buttered bread, cut into wing shapes.

 Dear God, thank you for giving us the things we need. Amen

The 'it's not me' angel

FROM NUMBERS 22:1–35

Stephanie was sitting on George's bed. They were playing with George's bucking donkey game. George had won twice—mainly because he sent all the pieces flying by wriggling his toes just at the wrong moment when it was Stephanie's go.

Stephanie was getting cross. 'George! You're doing it on purpose!' she snapped, as the small plastic shapes were flung once again across the room. 'It's not me, it's the donkey!' shouted George.

Mum could hear the quarrel starting and came upstairs. 'I know someone else who thought that,' she said, 'but it wasn't the donkey's fault at all.

'God's people travelled across the desert for many years. At last, the land God had promised them was in sight. But the neighbours were worried. Who were these strangers? There were so many of them—far too many to fight.

'The king had an idea. If the strangers became ill and died, then he wouldn't have to fight them. Balaam was the man for the job. He could put a curse on them.

'Balaam got on his donkey and set off along the road. He wasn't happy about the job—but the pay was too good to miss.

'But God sent his angel with a message for Balaam. Three times the donkey saw the angel. Three times the donkey stopped. Balaam was furious. He beat the donkey with a stick.

'"It's not me, it's the donkey!" thought Balaam.

'"It's not me, it's the angel!" Balaam heard the donkey say.

'And then Balaam saw the angel too. The angel told him it was wrong to wish harm on God's people.'

Mum set the donkey game on the bedside table. 'In the Christmas story, King Herod asked the wise men to tell him where the baby was, because he wanted to harm Jesus,' she said.

She opened George's Bible to show them.

 'Go and make a careful search for the child, and when you find him, let me know.'
MATTHEW 2:8

To do

Play the card game *Donkey*, but play it so that the person left with the donkey card at the end of the game is the winner, not the loser. If you don't have the game, you could make the pairs from an ordinary pack of cards and use one of the jokers as the donkey card.

 Dear God, help us always to do the right thing. Amen

The 'only little' angel

FROM JUDGES 6:1–16

It was Saturday morning. George was off to play football. Stephanie was going to Brownies. When they got home they were going to put the Christmas tree up. George's bran tub angel was to sit at the very top.

George came back from football and flopped into a chair. 'We got beaten,' he moaned. 'The other team were much stronger than us.' Mum was setting the tree in its tub. 'I'm sure you did your best, George,' she said, one eye on his muddy shorts.

'Yes, but I'm only little.'

'That's what Gideon said when an angel came to see him,' said Mum. 'He can be our next Advent angel story.

'God's people had settled in the land that they had been promised. But they had a problem. Their neighbours were very strong. They kept stealing the crops and animals so that God's people had nothing to eat.

'Gideon was the youngest member of his family. His family belonged to the least important tribe in the whole of Israel. Gideon thought to himself, "I'm only little, what can I do?" Then one day Gideon had an idea. When the wheat was ready to be picked he hid some of it in an old winepress. The press was like a hollowed-out rock. It was a secret place.

'Gideon was busy threshing the wheat. Suddenly a voice behind him said, "The Lord is with you, brave and mighty man!" Gideon nearly jumped out of his skin.

'It was an angel with a message from God. God wanted Gideon to rescue his people from the thieves who were stealing their food. But the thieves were very strong. Gideon was only little, what could he do?

'"You can do it," said God, "because I will help you."'

Mum stepped back to look at the tree. 'In the Christmas story, Bethlehem was the least important town in the whole of Israel, but it is where Jesus was born,' she said.

She opened George's Bible to show him.

 Bethlehem, you are one of the smallest towns… but out of you I will bring a ruler, whose family line goes back to ancient times.
Micah 5:2

To do

Take an empty matchbox and fill it with the very smallest things that you can find. Think of the use each item has. In what way is it important?

 Dear God, thank you that we can do things for you, even when we are very small. Amen

Woken by an angel

FROM 1 KINGS 19:1–9

It was Sunday morning. George was nowhere to be seen. Only the very tips of his curly hair were peeping out from under the duvet.

Stephanie called to him on her way down to breakfast. There was no reply. Mum called to him on her way to make the beds. Still no sound came from George.

Mum fetched George's breakfast and went upstairs. She set down the tray and gave the duvet a gentle shake. 'Didn't you hear us calling you, George?' she asked.

'I heard you calling, but I don't want to get up,' he said. 'I don't want to be in the Christmas play. It's too much.'

Mum sat down on the edge of the bed. George looked very unhappy. 'It makes me all nervous,' he explained.

Mum sighed. 'You can sit with me and watch, if you like. No one will mind if you don't want to take part.

'Our Advent angel story today is about a man called Elijah. He was feeling very unhappy. "It's too much," he said, and he hid himself away. But an angel came to find him. "Wake up and eat," said the angel. The angel helped Elijah to see that God didn't expect him to do more than he could. The angel gave Elijah food to eat and the strength to carry on.'

'The Christmas story is like that. God doesn't expect you to do more than you can. But he would like you to be there. He invited the shepherds to come, but they didn't have to do anything.'

She opened George's Bible to show him. Then she left him to have his breakfast and think about things.

'Let's go to Bethlehem and see this thing that has happened, which the Lord has told us.'
LUKE 2:15

To do

Make a list of all the things you can do. Think of ways you could use the things on your list to help other people.

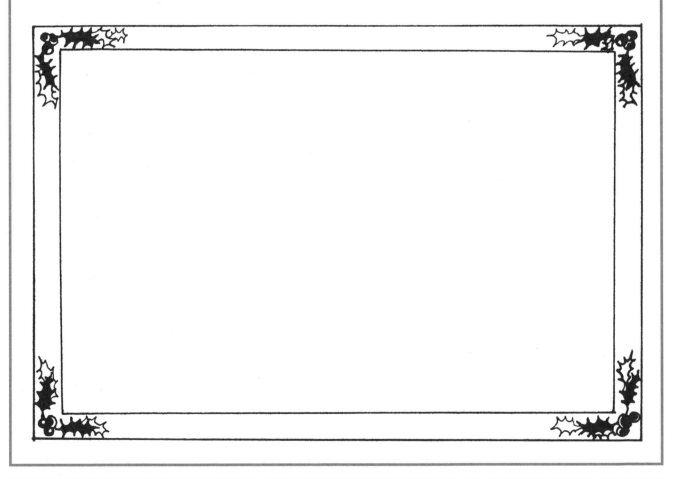

 Dear God, thank you for showing us that we can come to you just as we are. Amen

Angel songs

FROM PSALM 148:1–2

Monday morning was Stephanie's favourite morning. It was school choir practice day. Stephanie loved singing in the choir.

She jumped out of bed, humming to herself. They were practising for the carol service. 'Ding dong! merrily on high' was one of her favourites, particularly the angels' song bit that went, 'Glo…o…o…o…o…ria'. She got quite carried away with that.

Mum heard Stephanie humming.

'There's a song in the Bible about all God's angels,' she said. 'It can be our Advent angel story for today.'

Mum got George's picture Bible and opened it at Psalms. 'Here we are,' she said, 'number 148.' She read out the verse.

'Praise the Lord from heaven,
you that live in the heights above.
Praise him, all his angels,
all his heavenly armies.'

Stephanie looked over Mum's shoulder at the words. 'That's like the Christmas angels,' she said. 'They praised God, too.'

They looked at the Bible passage together. Before she went to school, Stephanie marked the place in her own Bible.

 Suddenly a great army of heaven's angels appeared with the angel, singing praises to God.
LUKE 2:13

To do

Make an acrostic poem of the word ANGELS. Look at the one on page 4 if you get stuck. Perhaps you could think up a tune to go with your poem.

A
N
G
E
L
S

 Dear God, thank you for giving us voices to sing your praises. Amen

Three friends and an angel

FROM DANIEL 3:1–30

Stephanie and George were very excited. Today was the day of the Christmas pantomime. Stephanie's Brown Owl had arranged for the Brownies to go, and younger brothers and sisters were invited too. They were meeting outside the theatre after school.

That evening, George told Mum all about it.

'You should have seen the treasures in the cave,' he said. 'Gold and silver and jewels and things. Aladdin got very rich!'

Mum smiled. 'I know a golden Advent angel story,' she said. 'It's about the friends of a young man called Daniel. We'll have it as our bedtime story.

'Daniel and his three friends worked in the royal court of Nebuchadnezzar, king of Babylon. The king was full of his own importance. He built a golden statue of himself, three times taller than a house and twice as wide as a tree. It could be seen for miles around. Everyone came to look.

'The king's herald made an announcement. "People of Babylon," he shouted. "When you hear the loud music, you must bow down and worship the statue of your king."

'The trumpets blew. The flutes, horns, pipes and harps trilled and tooted. Everyone bowed down. Everyone, that is, except Daniel's three friends. They would only bow down to God.

'The king was furious. "Throw them in the hottest fiery furnace you can find," he screamed.

'The three friends were tied up and thrown into the flames. The king came along to watch. Suddenly, he leapt to his feet. He could see *four* men walking unharmed in the flames, and one of the men was an angel. He flung open the furnace door. Out stepped Daniel's friends. God's angel had kept them safe.

'In the Christmas story, the wise men brought gold as a present for Jesus,' said Mum. 'They knew that Jesus was a king.'

She opened George's Bible to show him.

 They went into the house, and when they saw the child with his mother Mary, they knelt down and worshipped him. They brought out their gifts of gold, frankincense, and myrrh, and presented them to him.
MATTHEW 2:11

To do

Think of a present that you would like to give King Jesus. It doesn't have to be something you would buy in the shops.

 Dear King Jesus, help us to put you first in everything we do. Amen

Dreaming of angels

FROM DANIEL 4:1–17

George was writing his Christmas list. He tongue was curled over his top lip. He was thinking very hard. Suddenly he looked up. The list was finished. He was feeling very pleased with himself.

Stephanie was cutting out and colouring an angel for the Christmas tree. Each day they added an angel from the story. The tree was beginning to look great.

Mum came to see what they were doing. She helped Stephanie to hang the angel on the tree and looked at George's list.

'King Nebuchadnezzar made a list,' she said. 'It was a "thinking" list of all the wonderful things he had done. He was a very successful king.

'Then one night he had a dream. In his dream he saw a wonderful tree. It was big and beautiful and full of fruit. Animals rested in its shade. Birds nested in its branches. Its fruit was sweet and juicy and good to eat.

'Suddenly an angel came down from heaven. The angel ordered the tree to be cut down. Only the stump was left. The angel told the king that he would be like the tree stump, cut down and helpless and good for nothing. The angel wanted the king to learn that God is more important than kings.

'It took Nebuchadnezzar many years to learn his lesson. Slowly he learnt to praise God. "Everything the King of heaven does is right and just," he said. "He can humble anyone who acts proudly."'

Suddenly George had a thought. 'Jesus only had three presents!' he said. He took his list. He did quite a bit of crossing out.

'There!' said George.

Mum smiled. 'In the Christmas story there is a very special present,' she said. 'Can you see what it is?'

She fetched George's picture Bible and opened it to show them.

The shepherds hurried off and found Mary and Joseph and saw the baby lying in the manger.

Luke 2:16

To do

Make a Christmas list. Then cross out all the things you have thought of except three.

 Dear Jesus, thank you that you are the best present of all. Amen

An angel in the den

FROM DANIEL 6:1–28

George's best friend, Sam, came to tea after school. George and Sam had squash and biscuits. They watched television. They played on the computer. Then they got bored. George had an idea. They went upstairs and made a den under the desk in George's bedroom. It was great fun.

'Can we have tea in our den?' George asked Mum.

After Sam had gone, Mum helped George clear away the den. 'There's a den in our story today,' she said. 'It's another story about Daniel.

'Daniel had worked in the royal courts for many years. When he was old, a new king ruled over Babylon. King Darius liked Daniel, but his advisers were very jealous.

'One day the king's advisers had an idea. They thought up a new law. The law said that anyone who wanted anything must ask the king. The king thought this was a good law and he signed it with his royal seal.

'The next day, Daniel was saying his prayers, asking God for everything, just as he always did. The advisers went to the king. "Daniel has broken the new law," they said. "He must be thrown to the lions." The king sighed. He knew he had been tricked.

'King Darius ordered Daniel to be thrown to the lions. "May your God, whom you serve so loyally, rescue you," he said.

'That night the king couldn't sleep. In the morning he got up and went to the lions' den. And there was Daniel, safe and well! God had sent his angel to shut the lions' mouths!

'King Darius ordered Daniel to be brought out of the den and the advisers to be thrown in instead. This time there was no angel to shut the lions' mouths.

'The Christmas story is really about how God came to rescue us,' said Mum, tucking George up snug and warm in his bed.

She opened George's Bible to show him. Then she left him to dream of angels and lions and Christmas.

 'Mary will have a son, and you will name him Jesus—because he will save his people from their sins.'
MATTHEW 1:21

To do

• Cut a 15cm square of strong card from a cereal box.

• Make a maze by arranging some paper straws on the square. Cut them to fit and glue them in place.

• Draw a lion in the middle of the maze and an angel at the exit.

• Starting at the middle, use a marble to find your way out of the maze.

 Dear God, thank you that you are always with us. Amen

The 'getting ready' angel

FROM LUKE 1:11

George woke up early. Something was making his tummy tingle. He leapt out of bed and ran into Stephanie's bedroom. He bounced on her bed. Stephanie woke up with a yell.

'George! Get off! What do you think you're doing?'

George had remembered why he had a tingle in his tummy. There was no school today. It was Christmas shopping day. They were catching the bus into town.

Mum came to see what all the noise was about. 'You're an early messenger, George!' she said. 'I think we'll have a "getting ready" story today—but not quite *this* early in the morning, please!'

The bus jerked and rumbled its way into town. There was a lot of traffic and plenty of time for a story.

'Once there was an old priest called Zechariah,' said Mum, raising her voice against the noise of the engine. 'Zechariah knew all about God's promises to rescue his people. Every day he prayed that it would happen.

'One day, Zechariah was all alone in the temple. Suddenly an angel came and stood beside him. It was God's "getting ready" angel. The angel told the old priest that his wife, Elizabeth, was going to have a baby boy called John. When the baby was grown up, he would get everything ready for Jesus.

'Zechariah was all of a dither. First his knees knocked with fear, then his teeth chattered with fright. "I… I… I don't believe you!" he stammered. But it *was* true! Elizabeth was expecting a baby! And they called the baby John, just as the angel had said.'

'The angel's name was Gabriel,' said Mum. 'When we get home I'll show you the story in the Bible where he comes to visit Zechariah.'

 'Don't be afraid, Zechariah! God has heard your prayer, and your wife Elizabeth will bear you a son. You are to name him John… He will get the Lord's people ready for him.'
LUKE 1:13 AND 17

To do

Help the birds get ready for winter. You'll need a small packet of birdseed, an open pine cone, peanut butter and some string or ribbon.

• Mix the peanut butter with the seeds.

• Push the mixture into the cone.

• Tie the string or ribbon round the tip of the cone and hang it from a branch.

 Dear God, help us to get ready for you. Amen

14

Gabriel goes to Nazareth

FROM LUKE 1:26–38

Mum was in the kitchen making a Christmas cake. George was helping. There was cake mixture on his nose and in his hair. Best of all, there was cake mixture in his tummy.

'Perhaps Mary was doing some baking when the angel Gabriel came to see her,' said Mum.

'Gabriel is the true Advent angel. Some time after he had given Zechariah God's message, he went to see Mary. I think he gave Mary a bit of a shock. It's not every day you expect to see an angel in your kitchen.

'Gabriel spoke gently to her. "Peace be with you!" he said. "The Lord is with you and has greatly blessed you!"

'Gabriel's message for Mary was the most wonderful news of all. It was the news that Jesus was to be born. And Mary was to be his mother. Gabriel told Mary that Elizabeth was also expecting a baby. Elizabeth and Mary were cousins.

'"There is nothing that God cannot do," said Gabriel.

'"I am the Lord's servant," said Mary; "may it happen to me as you have said."'

George went to fetch his picture Bible and Mum showed him where to find the story of Gabriel, the true Advent angel.

God sent the angel Gabriel to a town in Galilee named Nazareth. He had a message for a young woman. Her name was Mary.
LUKE 1:26–27

To do

Look back to the first three days to find the stories that mention the three things that were said when Gabriel visited Mary.

• Fold a sheet of A4 paper in half along its length. Fold this strip in half widthways, then fold the two ends back on themselves. Open out to make a concertina-style book.

• Make the left-hand section the cover and draw a picture of Gabriel visiting Mary. On each of the remaining three sections draw a picture from the stories in which Gabriel and Mary's words appear.

 Dear God, thank you for sending your angel to Nazareth with such wonderful news. Amen

The encouraging angel

FROM MATTHEW 1:18–25

It was the day of the Christmas nativity. Stephanie was Mary. She had learnt her lines very carefully and knew them by heart. George was the innkeeper. It was his job to fill the crib with real hay. His best friend, Sam, was Joseph.

The children came to church in their costumes. There was a buzz of excitement in the air. Sam's little brother, Jack, had a tea-towel on his head. He was hiding behind his mum. He didn't want to join in.

George remembered how he hadn't wanted to join in. But it was all right now.

After the service, the family walked home together. 'Our angel story today is about Joseph,' said Mum. 'Joseph is someone who didn't want to join in.

'Mary and Joseph were planning to get married. Then Mary told him what the angel had said. Joseph was very upset. Mary was having a baby and he wasn't the father. Perhaps he shouldn't marry her after all. That night Joseph tossed and turned in his sleep.

'Suddenly, Joseph saw an angel standing by the bed. "Don't worry, Joseph," said the angel, "everything will be all right." Joseph woke up. He was feeling much happier. Now he knew God wanted him to marry Mary and help her care for baby Jesus—the son of God.'

When they got home, George fetched his picture Bible. Mum opened it right at the beginning of the New Testament and showed him the story of Joseph and the angel.

An angel of the Lord appeared to Joseph in a dream and said, 'Joseph, descendant of David, do not be afraid to take Mary to be your wife.'
MATTHEW 1:20

To do

Make an angel mobile.

• Photocopy the basic angel shape three times, making each one slightly smaller than the one before. Now photocopy again so that you have two copies of each size.

• Glue all the angel shapes on to thin card. Cut out each one.

• Take a long length of thread. Using a small piece of sticky tape, stick one end of the thread down the middle of one of the largest angel shapes. Sandwich the thread by gluing the other large angel shape over the first, covering the thread and sticky tape.

• Leaving a short length of thread between each angel, repeat with the middle-sized angel and the smallest angel.

• With the smallest angel, loop the thread back on itself and cut the end before you tape it down. This will make a hanger for your mobile.

• Write the words *Do not be afraid* on the largest angel.

• Colour in your mobile and hang it up.

 Dear God, help us to listen to what you have to say when we feel upset. Amen

16

An angel at midnight

FROM LUKE 2:8–12

There was a strange white light in the bedroom. Everything was very quiet. George woke up. He jumped out of bed and opened the curtains. Snow! It had been snowing all night. Everything was snuggled under a deep, white blanket.

Mum was busy seeking out hats and scarves and gloves. George's wellington boots stood ready by the door.

'It must have been very cold last night,' said Mum, 'to have snowed so hard.

'Our angel story today is about a very cold night. It happened when some shepherds were out in the fields, looking after their sheep.

'The shepherds lit a fire. They huddled together in its warmth, telling stories and keeping watch for wild animals. They were used to guarding their sheep in the deep, dark night.

'Suddenly, the sky was filled with a blaze of light. The shepherds were terrified. Then they saw the angel.

'Their terror turned to amazement…

'…their amazement turned to wonder…

'…their wonder turned to joy…

'…when they heard the angel's message.'

Mum smiled. 'The good news of Jesus melted away all their fear,' she said.

This time it was Stephanie's turn to find the story in the Bible. Mum helped her to find Luke's Gospel.

The angel said to them, 'Don't be afraid! I am here with good news for you, which will bring great joy to all the people.'

LUKE 2:10

To do

Start with the first letter at the top of the outside ring, then use every third letter to find out what happened when the angel came to the shepherds. Unscramble the letters in the centre of the circle to find the angel's message.

Answer: Luke 2:9

Dear God, thank you for the good news of Jesus. Amen

A host of angels

FROM LUKE 2:13–15

It was the day of the school carol service. Stephanie was bubbling with excitement. Snatches of 'Angels from the realms of glory' could be heard floating through the bathroom door. The pauses between the words indicated that Stephanie was cleaning her teeth.

The carol service was due to start at seven o'clock. George yawned. He didn't normally stay up that late.

'Why does the song say *angels* from the realms of glory?' he asked Mum. 'Most of our stories have only had *one* angel.'

'That's the next part of the shepherds' story,' said Mum. 'At first they saw only one angel. He told them that Jesus had been born. Then suddenly the sky was filled with hundreds and hundreds of angels. The air was full of singing. The angels sang praises to God for the birth of baby Jesus.'

'That can be our angel story for today!' said George. 'Lots of them!'

He ran to fetch his picture Bible and they found the place together.

'We sing carols because we want to say 'thank you' to God for Jesus, just as the angels did,' said Mum. 'Can you see what they sang?'

'Glory to God in the highest heaven, and peace on earth to those with whom he is pleased!'

Luke 2:14

To do

Make an angel Christmas card and send it to a friend.

• Take a piece of thin card measuring 35cm by 12cm. Fold it every 5cm like a concertina. Fold up the card and press it flat.

• Trace the basic angel shape on to the front. All the points marked 'x' should touch the edges of the card. Cut round the shape.

• Open out to show a host of angels. Colour the angels.

• Write *Glory to God in the highest heaven* along the bottom of the card, placing one word on each section.

Dear God, thank you for Christmas. Thank you for Jesus. Amen

18

Guardian angels

FROM PSALM 91:11–12

It was Mum's birthday. Stephanie and George had been saving their pocket money for weeks, to buy her a new album. Mum and Stephanie prepared the birthday tea. There was pizza and trifle and birthday cake. Mum sang along to her birthday present.

'For you and I have a guardian angel,
On high with nothing to do…'

Finally, the table was laid and everything was ready.

'Mum.' Stephanie was munching her way through a large slice of birthday cake. 'What are guardian angels?'

Mum paused. George's share of the cake was balanced in mid-air on her knife.

'We've had lots of stories about angels being God's special messengers,' she said. 'But the Bible tells us that angels guide and protect us, too. They are our guardian angels.'

George held his plate up for the slice of cake. 'I know a prayer about that,' he said. 'It's in the book of prayers that Gran gave me.'

Stephanie knew the prayer too. They said it together.

'Before I lay me down to sleep,
I pray the Lord my soul to keep.
Four corners to my bed,
Four angels there are spread.'

Mum laughed. 'Well done, you two—that's a good prayer to say before you go to bed.' After tea, George and Stephanie helped clear away. Then they found the place in George's Bible where it said that God's angels protect us, and they played an 'angel' game.

God will put his angels in charge of you to protect you wherever you go. They will hold you up with their hands to keep you from hurting your feet on the stones.

PSALM 91:11–12

To do

Starting with the letter 'A', think of a word to describe angels, using every letter of the alphabet. For instance, you could start with 'Angels are… amazing!' If you are playing the game with friends, take it in turns to think of a word.

 Dear God, thank you for your angels who protect and guide us. Amen

19

Angel thoughts

FROM MATTHEW 2:1–12

It was the last day of term. George and Stephanie came out of school laden with their share of the cleared classrooms. Paintings and models, books and Christmas cards spilt from their school bags and their arms.

George managed to free a hand when they reached the main road. He curled his fingers around Mum's. They looked and listened, and crossed together.

'Did angels protect Jesus when he was a baby?' he asked. 'Oh, yes!' said Mum. 'Jesus was born in the country of Judea during the time when Herod was king. When the wise men turned up at the royal palace looking for the baby king, Herod was very upset. He was king! He didn't want anyone else to take his place!

'Herod had a plan! He found out where Jesus had been born. He called the wise men to a secret meeting. He sent them to Bethlehem to find the baby. He asked them to come back with directions so that he could visit the baby too. The wise men didn't realize that Herod planned to kill baby Jesus.

'But God had a plan, too! After the wise men had visited baby Jesus, God spoke to them in a dream. We're not told he sent an angel this time. But sometimes in our stories when the angel speaks, God speaks. Perhaps it was like this for the wise men.'

When they got home, George fetched his Bible. They looked together at the story of the visitors from the east. Stephanie read out the bit about the dream.

Then they returned to their own country by another road, since God had warned them in a dream not to go back to Herod.
MATTHEW 2:12

To do

Make a wise man finger puppet.

Photocopy the three wise men. Colour them in, and cut them out. Fold the two outer edges round till they fit the top of your finger, and fasten the back with a piece of sticky tape.

OR: You can make your own wise man with the blank image. Photocopy the shape three times and draw in whatever you think the wise men might have looked like.

Dear God, help us to listen to your voice. Amen

47

20

Angel directions

FROM MATTHEW 2:13–15

Everyone was busy in the kitchen. George and Stephanie were making Christmas sweets—some to wrap as presents, some to hang from the tree in tiny baskets, ready for Christmas Day. Mum was making mince pies.

George was in charge of the chocolate vermicelli. He swirled a sweet into its chocolate jacket and suddenly had a thought.

'Did Herod find baby Jesus?' he asked.

'Oh, no,' said Mum. 'God continued to protect his baby son. This can be our angel story for today.

'After the wise men had given their presents to Jesus, they did as God had asked in their dream. They went straight back home. They didn't go to Jerusalem. They didn't visit King Herod.

'That same night, Joseph too had a dream. He dreamt about an angel. The angel warned him that Herod was planning to kill baby Jesus. The angel told Joseph to take his young family far away from Bethlehem. Not to another village, not to another town, but to another country. A country called Egypt.

'Joseph woke Mary. They snuggled Jesus safe and warm. In the deep, dark night they left the little town of Bethlehem. They travelled for many miles. When they got to Egypt they stayed, quietly waiting until it was safe to go back home.'

George's picture Bible lay open on the kitchen table. 'All our stories at the moment come from the beginning of Matthew's Gospel,' said Mum.

 Joseph got up, took the child and his mother, and left during the night for Egypt, where he stayed until Herod died.
MATTHEW 2:14

To do

Make some Christmas truffles.

• Break 125g of plain chocolate into a heat-resistant bowl. Gently melt the chocolate in a microwave, or over a pan of water. Ask an adult to help.

• Take off the heat. Add two tablespoons of blackcurrant squash and beat in 30g of butter. Add 50g of sieved icing sugar and 50g of ground almonds, and mix until well blended.

• Leave until the mixture is firm enough to handle. Divide into about sixteen even-sized pieces. Roll each piece into a ball.

• Put some chocolate vermicelli into a small bowl. Swirl each truffle in the bowl until it is well coated.

• Put into a small sweet-paper case and press half a glacé cherry on the top.

 Dear God, thank you for looking after baby Jesus. Amen

The 'going home' angel

FROM MATTHEW 2:19–23

Stephanie and George were very excited. Gran and Grandpa were coming to stay for Christmas. George tidied his toys. Stephanie polished the furniture. Mum hoovered the carpets. Soon everything was ready.

Gran and Grandpa arrived in time for lunch. Mum helped Grandpa to carry in the suitcases. No one was allowed to see the secret parcels tucked away in the boot of the car.

Gran and Grandpa spotted the Christmas tree as soon as they stepped indoors. They wanted to know all about the Advent angels. George and Stephanie showed them how each angel was holding a special object, which was part of the story.

'After King Herod died, Joseph had another dream,' said Mum. 'Once again he saw an angel. The angel said it was time to go back home—back to their family and friends. Joseph was very excited. Mary tidied the house. Joseph cleaned and polished. Soon everything was ready. Closing the door behind them, they set out on their journey.

'But Joseph was worried. Yes, King Herod was dead, but his son ruled in his place. Perhaps it still was not safe to live in Bethlehem.

'Joseph had another dream. This time, an angel told Joseph to take his family to Nazareth, far away from the ears and eyes of King Archelaus.

'So Joseph made his home in Nazareth. He set up his carpenter's shop and settled down quietly to look after his little family.'

George fetched his picture Bible and showed Gran and Grandpa how they had heard angel stories each day, right from the beginning of Advent. Then he found Joseph's 'going home' story.

 After Herod died, an angel of the Lord appeared in a dream to Joseph in Egypt and said, 'Get up, take the child and his mother, and go back to the land of Israel, because those who tried to kill the child are dead.'
MATTHEW 2:19–20

To do

Make an angel bookmark for your favourite book, or to give as a present.

• Photocopy the bookmark pattern on to thin card.

• Photocopy the small angel shape on to thin card. Colour both the card and the angel.

• Decorate using silver or gold pens, star shapes or glitter glues. Do not colour or decorate the shaded area on the bookmark.

• Stick the angel to the card in the position shown.

 Dear God, help us to get ready to welcome you into our homes and our hearts at Christmas. Amen

22

Greater than angels

FROM HEBREWS 1:1–14

There were just a few days left until Christmas Day. Mum and Stephanie had gone shopping with Gran. Grandpa and George were making an angel decoration for the centre of the Christmas table.

'Angels are great!' said George. 'They're the best!'

'But not as great as Jesus,' said Grandpa. 'Jesus is the very best of all!'

George looked at his Grandpa. So many angel stories, but *he'd* never seen one. What did Grandpa know about them?

Grandpa scratched his head. 'Angels are God's heavenly servants, George,' he said. 'We can't see them unless God chooses that we should. Angels are happiest when they are worshipping God. The songs of a trillion-billion angel voices echo round his heavenly throne.

'But Jesus is God's son. He is the exact likeness of God—greater than the greatest angel. He is like a light that reflects the brightness of God's glory.

'That's what Christmas is all about, George,' he said. 'It's the time when we celebrate the birthday of God's very own son.'

Grandpa put the finishing touches to the angel decoration. Then he opened George's Bible and showed him what it said.

The Son was made greater than the angels, just as the name that God gave him is greater than theirs… When God was about to send his first-born Son into the world, he said: 'All God's angels must worship him.'

HEBREWS 1:4 AND 6

To do

Make an angel decoration for the Christmas table.

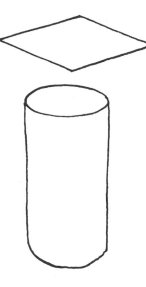

• Make a candle by cutting a 12cm-high section from a card roll. The middle of a kitchen roll would be ideal.

• Cut a square of strong paper, large enough to cover the top of one end of the tube. Fix in place with sticky tape.

• Cut a 16cm square of Christmas paper or make your own design on a piece of plain paper.

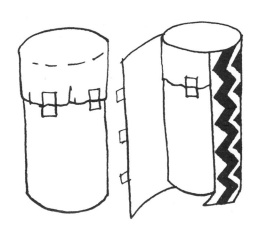

• Placing the top of the paper at the top of the tube, wrap around and secure with sticky tape. Tuck the bottom end inside the tube.

• Draw a flame shape on thin card. Cut it out and colour it in. Make a small slit in the middle of the top of the candle and push the flame into the slit.

• Decorate the border of a paper plate with a Christmas design. Tape the candle to the centre of the plate.

• Cut out eight small angel shapes and colour in. Fold back the bottom 2cm of the angel's skirt and stick the angels around the edge of your border.

 Dear God, help us to worship you in all we do. Amen

The 'not quite' angels

FROM HEBREWS 2:6–8 AND PSALM 8

It was a fine sunny morning, crisp and bright. George was very excited. Soon it would be Christmas Day. He was making a lot of noise. Mum looked tired. So much noise made her head ache! Gran looked up from her knitting.

'It's such a lovely morning, I think we'll go for a walk,' she said. 'George and Stephanie can play postman and deliver the local Christmas cards.'

Outside, frost sparkled on the grass. A pair of magpies chattered in a tree. A pot of winter pansies nodded their heads in the sun. Gran gave a sigh as she watched the children pop the last card through the last letterbox.

'It's a beautiful morning,' she said. 'The sort of morning made to praise God.'

Stephanie gave a little hop, skip and jump. 'I wish I could be an angel and join in the singing,' she said.

'That's silly!' said George. 'We're not angels!'

Gran smiled. 'Not *so* silly,' she said. 'The Bible tells us that God made us lower than angels, but crowned us with glory and honour. Part of the meaning of Christmas is that Jesus has made it possible for us to praise God alongside the angels,' she said. 'And even now, God hears us when we sing to him.'

When they got home, Gran opened George's Bible and showed the children the 'not quite angels' song.

O Lord, our Lord, your greatness is seen in all the world! Your praise reaches up to the heavens; it is sung by children and babies.
PSALM 8:1–2

To do

Make a robin decoration for the Christmas tree.

• With a pair of nail scissors, carefully cut an oval in the shell of an egg. Ask an adult to help you. Remove the insides of the egg and wash the shell thoroughly.

• Paint the shell with poster paint and leave to dry.

• Use a needle to draw a length of silver thread through the top of the shell. Pass the needle back through the shell and knot the two ends of the thread on the inside of the shell. Glue or tape to secure.

• Glue around the edge of the oval and decorate with lace, glitter or sequins.

• Mix a little flour with some water and glue to make a paste. Place in the bottom of the oval and press a robin Christmas cake decoration into the paste. Leave until completely dry.

• Hang the decoration on your tree.

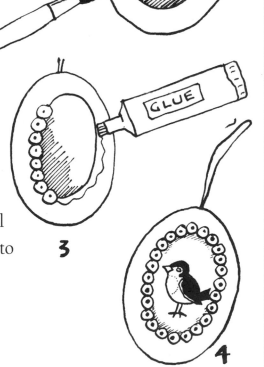

Dear God, thank you for the world. Help us to look after all the things you have created. Amen

24

Just as the angels said

FROM LUKE 2:15–20

It was Christmas Eve. There was to be a crib service in the church. Lots and lots of people would be there. George was impatient to go. He wanted to be as near the crib as possible.

The vicar told everyone about the shepherds. The shepherds had told Mary and Joseph about the angels. George remembered the story.

The vicar said that everyone had been amazed when they heard the shepherds' story. George wasn't amazed. He leaned forward to look more closely at the crib scene. There were Joseph and Mary and the shepherds.

The vicar said that Mary remembered everything in her heart and thought deeply about it all. George looked at Mary. There was a kind, gentle smile on her face. She was looking at the baby.

The vicar said that the shepherds went back to their fields, singing praises to God for all they had heard and seen. George thought about all the angel stories he had heard.

The vicar said that angels were God's special messengers. George thought of his little bran tub angel, sitting on top of the tree at home. He thought of all the angels he and Stephanie had made together and hung in the branches of the tree.

The vicar said that everything had happened just as the angel had told them. George looked into the crib. The tiny baby smiled up at him.

George smiled back at the baby. A tinge of excitement crept into his tummy. Someone was reading from the Bible.

 The shepherds went back, singing praises to God for all they had heard and seen; it had been just as the angel had told them.
LUKE 2:20

To do

Make some angel paper and use it to write your 'thank you' letters after Christmas.

• Trace a row of small angel shapes on to a strip of thin card and carefully cut the angel shapes out of the middle of the strip to make a stencil.

• Tape the stencil firmly across a piece of plain writing paper. Fill the angel-shaped holes with paint. Allow to dry and then carefully peel away the stencil.

• Repeat to make borders and headings for each sheet of paper.

 Dear God, thank you for the present of Christmas. Thank you that Jesus came just as you promised he would. Amen

How to make your very own Advent Angel

1. Fold a sheet of medium-weight card measuring 22cm x 14cm in half widthways and trace the basic angel shape on to one side. Cut out both pieces. Leave to one side.

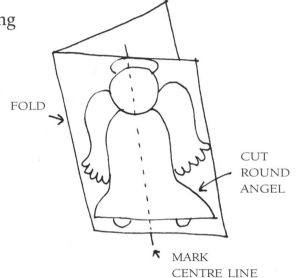

FOLD

CUT ROUND ANGEL

MARK CENTRE LINE

2. Take six pieces of paper, two silver, two gold and two white, measuring 10cm x 14cm. Fold each separate piece in half and in half again.

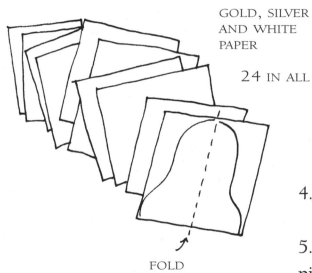

GOLD, SILVER AND WHITE PAPER

24 IN ALL

FOLD

3. Trace the bell shape on each piece of paper. Cut out the shape. You should have eight bells in each of the three colours.

4. Fold each bell shape in half.

5. Open the bell shapes and put them in two piles, with four of each colour in each pile.

6. Interleaf the colours in each pile (silver, gold, white and so on) until all the pieces are used up.

7. Take one pile, and staple the bell shapes together along the fold. Make sure the staples lie exactly on the fold.

8. Mark the centre line of the angel shape, using a pencil.

STAPLE

9. Take the first pile and glue the back of the bottom bell. Stick on to the angel shape, lining the edges up accurately. The centre lines should match exactly. Allow to dry.

10. Using double-sided sticky tape, tape the bell shapes to each other as follows:

11. Start with the bottom left-hand side of the bell glued to the angel shape. Apply a small piece of double-sided tape to the bottom and stick next bell to it. Apply a small piece of tape to the middle of this bell and stick the next bell to it. Continue taping the bells in this way, alternately placing the tape on the bottom and middle of the bells as you go.

12. Repeat steps 7–12 with the second pile of bell shapes and the second angel shape.

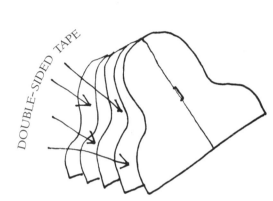

DOUBLE-SIDED TAPE

13. Glue the back of one of the angel shapes and carefully stick to the second angel, making sure that all edges are correctly aligned.

14. Cut the angel's hair out of white paper. Make the frills by cutting thin strips into the hair with scissors. Carefully curl the strands with the blade of the scissors. Glue the hair in place, leaving the halo free. Draw features on the angel's face.

PAPER CURLS

THE
FINISHED
ANGEL

Angel Objects

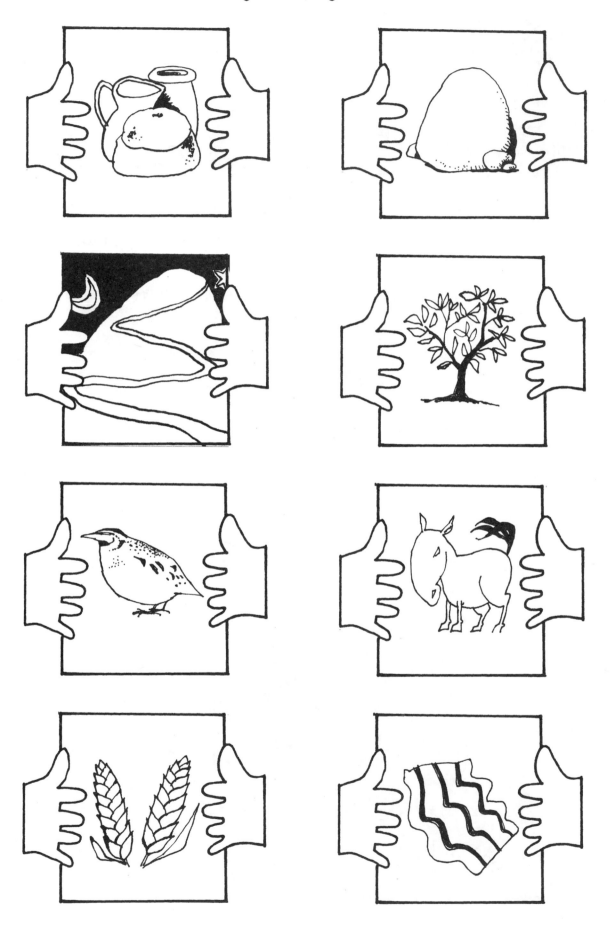

Basic angel shape

Photocopy the basic angel shape for use with the craft activities on pages 39 and 43, and use as the template for the Advent Angel model on pages 58–59.

Basic bell shape

Photocopy the basic bell shape and use as the template for the Advent Angel model on pages 58–59.

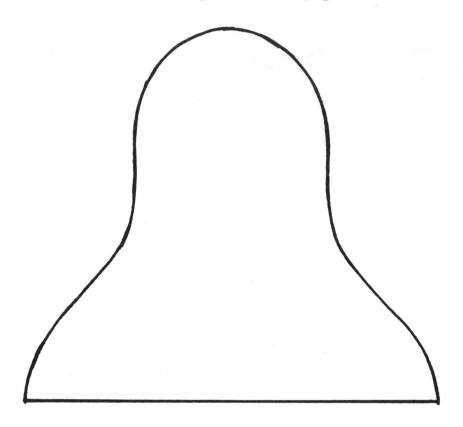

Small angel shape

Photocopy the small angel shape for use with the crafts on pages 15, 17, 51, 53 and 57.